LOVE

LETTERS

TO

GOD

LOVE LETTERS TO GOD

(A Guide to Building and Strengthening Your Relationship with God)

By

Yvonne Annette' Stroud

ISBN: 9781075613722

ACKNOWLEDGEMENTS

First and foremost, I give praise, honor, and glory to God Almighty. Without God's guidance, mercy, and grace, I could not have been able to accomplish anything in life. Second, I would like to thank my wonderful husband, Julius Stroud III, who has supported me from the moment we decided to become a couple, let alone husband and wife. He has been a God-send, and I appreciate all he has done to help me achieve my dreams. Next, I would like to thank my sons Julius IV, Jhan, and Jordan for your continued encouragement. I would also like to thank Pastor Ann Danner, my dear friend and Sister-in-Christ. Your guidance, support, and encouragement have been such a blessing to me. Thank you for allowing God to use you to open my eyes to what God has placed in me and desires to birth out of me. Finally, thank you to all who have prayed for me and encouraged me whenever you had the opportunity. You, too, are a blessing from God. It is my sincere prayer that God's favor will move mightily in all your lives. Keep on encouraging and uplifting everywhere you go.

TABLE OF CONTENTS

FOREWORD

Just as a building needs a solid foundation to stand the tests of high winds, heavy rains, floods, and other disasters, so does a relationship with God need a solid foundation to stand the tests of life: disappointment, failure, deception, worry, anxiety, stress, fear, depression, anger, rage, unforgiveness, and peer pressure to name a few.

That solid foundation needed for a relationship with God can only come when we first, repent of our sins. Second, surrender our lives to God. Third, allow God to take up residence in our hearts. More importantly, our relationship with God must be nurtured. We must spend time talking to God. Yes, God already knows how we feel, but He wants us to express our feelings openly to Him. In addition, time spent with God must be a priority. We make time for people we want to get to know better. Isn't God more important? OF COURSE! Therefore, make time to spend with Him, to get to know Him better, and to build a relationship of trust and hope with Him.

On this journey, reading and reflection of each poem will span three days. Additional pages have been provided to the back of the book if you need to add to your reflection or meditation notes. I encourage you to end each session in conversation with God and to complete each reflection task honestly. John 8:32 (KJV) says, "And ye shall know the truth and the truth shall make you free. Allow yourself to be freed.

As you venture through this journey, don't rush the process. Follow the daily plans being sure to revisit the poem each day. Allow yourself to fall deeply in love with God for the first time or all over again. Open up your heart to God. Speak to God from the depths of your soul. God's waiting. God's listening, and God's ready to build, strengthen, and solidify His relationship with you. Today, choose to start a new chapter of love in your life. Choose God. I did, and it was the best decision I have ever made! It has made all the difference in the world!

ARE TIRED OF CONTINUOUS FRUSTRATION, DOUBT, FEAR, AND ANGUISH?

ARE YOU READY FOR A BETTER LIFE?

ARE YOU READY TO BE FREED?

ARE YOU READY TO DRAW CLOSER TO GOD?

YES? THEN TURN THE PAGE AND BEGIN YOUR JOURNEY TO FREEDOM!

.

FIRST THINGS FIRST

Before you begin, list your goals for this journey. Next to each goal, write down why you hope to achieve it.

_____

_____

_____

_____

_____

_____

_____

_____

_____

_____

_____

_____

_____

_____

_____

_____

_____

_____

PART
1

For a Wretch Like Me

You left your Holy throne and took upon sin
To save a wretch like me.
You lived humbly but was criticized without-within,
But you endured it all for a wretch like me.

Questioned, mocked, betrayed by your own
All for a wretch like me.
Abandoned in your darkest hour-left alone
Yes, for a wretch like me.

Beaten, whipped to the brink of death
Just to save a wretch like me.
"Forgive them Father". "It is Finished" with your last breath
All to bring salvation to a wretch like me.

Thank you, Jesus, from the depths of my soul.

From,

A Wretch Undone

(Once lost - Now found - Now whole)

John 3:16 (KJV)
 For God so loved the world, that he gave his only begotten Son, that whosoever believeth in him should not perish, but have everlasting life.

THINK ABOUT THIS...

Over two thousand years ago Jesus gave His life for all. God knew the temptations of sin held us hostage. He knew we were too weak to fight them ourselves, and in the end, could never be able to live up to the demands of the Law, His commandments to His people. Because of God's compassion for His people, he sent his only son, Jesus, to die for their sins. But, not only for their sins, but for the sins of all mankind.

We as humans are not perfect in any way. No matter how hard we try to do the right thing all the time, we can't. The lusts of our flesh trap us. They lie to us. They entice us. Giving in to them puts us on the road to an eternal life of torment. So, in stepped Jesus to give his life as a final sacrifice to God for sin. It didn't matter how messed up mankind was (and still is) God loved us so much that He made a way for us to be freed from sin's hypnotic hold. We don't have to give in to the wrong that entices us on a daily basis. We have been given the power and authority over it. All we have to do is say "yes" to God. He loves us unconditionally, no matter the wrong we have done.

So, I encourage you to love God back. God is not like people, putting stipulations on His love for you. Remember, God's love is **unconditional**. God desires to have a relationship with you. He already loves you and has proven His love for you. He's waiting. His arms are outstretched. Will you run into them and let God wrap you in His love?

Take this time to thank God for saving your soul. If in this moment you have not given your life fully to God or have not given your life to God at all, then I want to invite you to confess your wrong (your sins) and ask God to forgive you. Ask Jesus to enter your heart and take charge of your life. This is today's focus. Remembering, recognizing, what God has done for you in spite of your sins, in spite of your faults. Don't rush this moment. Open your heart fully to God. He's waiting with arms stretched wide open.

ROMANS 10:9-10 (KJV)

9 That if thou shalt confess with thy mouth the Lord Jesus, and shalt believe in thine heart that God hath raised him from the dead, thou shalt be saved.

10 For with the heart man believeth unto righteousness; and with the mouth confession is made unto salvation.

Confession + Belief = Redemption

DAY 2 - REFLECTION

TASKS:

1. List everything you have ever done wrong. Think about what you may have said that was not right. Think about the mean and evil thoughts you've had. List it all, from your childhood up to this moment in your life.

   A little Heads Up for You: You might want to write your list horizontally instead of vertically. I guarantee you will probably have to come back and add more as the Holy Spirit continues to remind you of your past sins as it did me. I had already begun completing task #2 when I was reminded of more of my wrong. I ran out of room and had to continue my list in a separate space. It's amazing how we would like to forget our wrongs and think of ourselves as so good. Truth be told, we have ALL done a lot of wrong to God and others.

_____

_____

_____

_____

_____

_____

_____

_____

_____

_____

_____

2. Now, make a list of the good things you have done for others. Don't just include what you've done for those who treated you right. Include the good you've done for those who wronged you. I must caution you. God doesn't want you to list every time you did a good deed. God wants you to list the good deed. For example, you may have helped more than one person financially, but you can only list "financial support" which covers each time. It's not the number of times that's important here. It's the deed.

_____

_____

_____

_____

_____

_____

_____

_____

_____

Which list is longer? I'm guessing the first list. That's why God sent Jesus. We don't deserve God's mercy and grace, but He chooses to freely give them to us. This alone should give you the desire to spend more time with God and solidify your relationship with Him.

Take this moment to reach out to God. Reread the letter, and if need be, recommit to God.Talk to God openly and honestly and open up your heart to receive all God has for you. Most importantly, don't forget to thank God for everything He has done for you. It's a whole lot more than you think. And it all started with Christ giving His life for our sins.

9

DAY 3 - MEDITATION

Read this passage of scripture and meditate on it for a few minutes before answering the question that follows. Remember to end this session in prayer with God.

John 10:10 (KJV)- The thief cometh not, but for to steal, and to kill, and to destroy: I am come that they might have life, and that they might have it more abundantly.

What does this scripture mean to you?

_____

_____

_____

_____

_____

_____

_____

_____

_____

_____

_____

_____

You Were There

I could have lost my mind;
Fallen victim to despair, hopelessness, and dread.
I could have given into the thoughts and ideas,
And taken the path of the dead.
Gone, forgotten, no more breaths to take.
Never to gaze upon the sun again, never to awake.

But you were there to take hold my hand;
Guiding me back from a lifeless land.
You were there to wrap me in your endless Love;
Showering forgiveness, peace, and joy from Heaven above.

Pulling me from Hell's tormenting grasp;
Securing me with Salvation; sealing me with a righteous clasp.
You washed and purged me with the blood of the Lamb.
The Holy One – Emmanuel - The Great I Am.

Lord, you were there to prevent my lost
Way back then on that old rugged cross.
You knew I would need your unselfish sacrifice.
To redeem my soul, you paid the ultimate price.

So here I am broken, humbled, and grateful too.
Because YOU were there, not family nor friends-YOU
I am free, delivered, covered with mercy and grace.
By your strength I continue to run my Christian race.
Thank you, Lord, for always staying near.
I'm comforted-at peace- and have no fear.

Because
You were (and still are) there.

Psalms 9:9(KJV) The LORD also will be a refuge for the oppressed, a refuge in times of trouble.

THINK ABOUT THIS...

People will always let you down. Yes, even those closest to you. Why? Because they are human, not perfect. No one is perfect but God. No one can take care of all our problems like God. While our friends and family may love us and would do anything for us, they cannot solve all our problems. They may not be able to talk us out of despair's valley, or fear's dark alley, or angers' fiery lake. God, however, is always available to listen to our problems and help us in our time of need. He's that soft, still voice saying, 'Yes you can." "You **are** worth it." "You may not can handle it, but I can." God is the one saying, "It might look hopeless, but it really isn't".

So, I encourage you to listen to the voice of God cheering you on. Step aside and let God do all the work. All God needs for you to do is trust Him. Allow God to be your fortress, your strong rock. Let God deliver you from whatever has you discouraged, upset, worried, or afraid. Allow God's strength to take hold of you. God is right there with His hands held out to take your troubles from you. He's always there.

Reread the letter, but this time include all those times you were able to keep on going, hoping, living. Think about all those times when troubles worked themselves out. It was God working behind the scenes. You might have thought it was a coincidence, luck, or the work of a person or group of people. In reality, it was God. So, give God the praise. Tell God how much you appreciate Him. Open up your mouth and glorify God's name. In this moment, right now, forgetting everything and everyone that brings you down and looking to your Heavenly Father, pour out a praise of thanksgiving. Don't only thank God for what He has already done and is doing, but also thank God for the blessings to come. They will surely outweigh any obstacles that will rear their ugly heads.

And if this moment finds you lost or discouraged, allow God to lift your head. He's saying to you right now, that all is not lost. He's been waiting on you. He's been right there with you the whole time.

DAY 2 - REFLECTION

TASKS:

1. List all the times things worked out in your favor. Don't just think big. Think about **everything** good that has happened.

_____

_____

_____

_____

_____

_____

_____

_____

_____

_____

2. Draw a heart beside every event in which you thought the outcome would **not** be in your favor, in which you just knew things **wouldn't** work out for you.

3. Look at your list, focusing on the areas God showed up for you when you didn't think victory was possible. If I know my God, and I know I do, then you have at least one heart drawn, if not more.

God never sleeps. He is always there beside you, waiting to take care of every obstacle and challenge that comes your way. Can you feel Him? Do you see God's work in your life? If you analyze your list, then you can see His work. If you close your eyes, meditate on all God has done for you, and begin to thank Him for it, you will feel God's presence. You will feel God's touch as His peace overshadows you and His joy fills your heart.

Take this moment to bask in God's presence. Humble yourself before Him. Lay at God's feet and worship Him for His unconditional love; for His mercy and grace.

DAY 3 - MEDITATION

Read this scripture and meditate on it for a few minutes before answering the question that follows. Remember to end this session in prayer with God.

Psalm 18:2 (KJV)
The LORD is my rock, and my fortress, and my deliverer; my God, my strength, in whom I will trust; my buckler, and the horn of my salvation, and my high tower.

What does this scripture mean to you?

_____

_____

_____

_____

_____

_____

_____

_____

_____

_____

_____

_____

_____

_____

_____

A Very Present Help

A very present help you are, Oh Lord.
A very present help you are.

A very present help in trouble,
A very present help you are.
A very present help in sorrow,
A very present help you are.
A very present help in sickness,
A very present help you are.

A very present help you are, Oh Lord.
A very present help you are.

A very present help in despair,
A very present help you are.
A very present help in times of struggle,
A very present help you are.
A very present help in loneliness,
A very present help you are.

A very present help you are, Oh Lord.
A very present help you are.

A very present help in confusion,
A very present help you are.
A very present help in doubt,
A very present help you are.
A very present help during fear,
A very present help you are.

A very present help you are, Oh Lord.
A very present help you are.

Psalm 46:1 (KJV) God is our refuge and strength, a very present help in trouble.

17

Think About This...

In life we all will experience several curve balls coming at u. We will all feel like we've been sideswiped by an 18-wheeler. We will all engage in moments of helplessness, hopelessness, sorrow, anxiety, depression, worry, fear, doubt, hurt, jealousy, confusion, and anger. The list is endless. What do you do in these moments? Who do you turn to, if anyone? This list comprises some forms of attack Satan uses against anyone who serves God or even thinks about turning their life around and giving it to God. These feelings and emotions will get us into trouble every time we give in to them. If we're not careful to think before we react, we will find ourselves in a place we don't want to be: mind gone, life gone, freedoms taken away, and worst of all our soul eternally lost.

So, what do you do? Do you turn to a friend or family member? Do you look for support from your church family, your Pastor? Doing so can be better than giving in to your emotions. But what about those times when family, friends, or church members are not around? What do you do then? Hopefully, you turn to God. Hopefully you turn to God **first** and allow Him to direct you. In most cases, friends and family are not going to have the answers. Friends and family are not going to be able to calm us or console us. God is a present help at the very second you need it. God is a present help **before** you ever need it. God was there in the beginning of it. He's right there in the middle of it. And God will be there at the end of it. Therefore, why not be grateful for God's presence? Why not be grateful for the people God will have there just when you need an actual person to talk to? "Help, Lord"! This is all you need to say when life's troubles begin to overwhelm you. God will do the rest. You only need to stand in faith.

If this moment finds you in a place where you have not surrendered to God. Do it now. Take that leap of faith and watch God begin to help you through whatever struggles you face at this very moment. God **is** your answer to survival; your answer to not losing your mind or your soul. God **is** a very present help. Talk to God now. Open your heart to Him and be honest about EVERYTHING. Your help will come.

DAY 2 - REFLECTION

TASK: List areas in your life where you need God's help. Be specific about the kind of help you need. Be mindful to not be selfish or unholy in your requests.

_____

_____

_____

_____

_____

_____

_____

_____

_____

_____

_____

_____

Now, begin to thank God for His help with each situation. Read your requests aloud, standing in faith knowing God is doing exactly what you need Him to do. Take this moment to honor God with thanksgiving and appreciation. He deserves it.

DAY 3 – MEDITATION

Read the following passage of scripture and meditate on its words. Answer the question that follows. Remember to end this session in prayer with God.

Psalm 30 King (KJV)
1 I will extol thee, O LORD; for thou hast lifted me up, and hast not made my foes to rejoice over me.
2 O LORD my God, I cried unto thee, and thou hast healed me.
3 O LORD, thou hast brought up my soul from the grave: thou hast kept me alive, that I should not go down to the pit.
4 Sing unto the LORD, O ye saints of his, and give thanks at the remembrance of his holiness.
5 For his anger endureth but a moment; in his favour is life: weeping may endure for a night, but joy cometh in the morning.

What does this chapter from Psalms mean to you?

_____

_____

_____

_____

_____

_____

_____

_____

_____

My Soul

My soul is lost without you.

My soul requires to be guided by you.

My soul is desperate for a touch from you.

My soul hungers to be fed by you.

My soul yearns to be close to you.

My soul cries out to be comforted by you.

My soul rejoices in only you.

My soul sings praises unto you.

My soul is complete-whole-with you.

My soul yearns to rest eternally with you.

My Soul

Psalm 42:1-2 (KJV)

1 As the hart panteth after the water brooks, so panteth my soul after thee, O God.

2 My soul thirsteth for God, for the living God: when shall I come and appear before God?

Think About This...

So far, the letters have encouraged you to see the hand of God moving in your life. Now the gears shift to you longing for God, longing to be in God's presence, longing to feel God's gentle touch. The scripture compares this longing to a thirsty deer. Have you ever been thirsty? I mean **really** thirsty? Have you ever found yourself in a desperate state for something to drink? Maybe it was because you were in the hot sun. Maybe it was because you had just finished working out. Maybe it was because you just finished eating something that caused you to need a drink. Do you remember that desperate feeling you had? That feeling is the same feeling God wants us to have for Him. God desires to have a relationship with his creation. He doesn't want things between Him and us to be "I say... You do". God gives us the free will to choose to come into relationship with Him. God wants to talk with us. God wants to comfort us. God wants to hear us sing and laugh in His presence. God wants to take care of us more than any person could ever care for us.

So, do you desire to be so close to God you can hear Him speak? You can feel His presence? You can see Him moving in your life and the lives of others? I hope you do. The best thirst anyone can ever have is the thirst for the righteousness, love, favor, and presence of God in their lives. Matthew 5:6 says "Blessed are they which do hunger and thirst after righteousness: for they shall be filled." Do you want to be filled with God's goodness? Do you want to be filled with God's love? Do you want to be filled with God's joy? Are you hungry and thirsty for better? God says, "It's yours".

At this time, surrender your heart and mind to God. Clear your mind of idle thoughts and focus on drawing closer to God. You might begin by serenading God with a song or begin to lift your voice in adoration for who God is to you. Create a space where God can draw close to you and you draw closer to God.

DAY 2 - REFLECTION

TASKS:

1. Think about 3 worldly items you strongly desire to have. Write them down.

_____

_____

_____

_____

2. Think about what you would gain if you had these items. Write it down.

_____

_____

_____

_____

_____

_____

_____

_____

_____

How did you feel as you fantasized about having these items? I bet you were one happy camper. Now multiply that feeling times a million (which is still not enough). That's how elated you would be having a solid relationship with God.

Of course, you may get blindsided and thrown off your game from time to time, but the difference is that with a solid relationship with God, you will bounce back. Victory is always yours for the grabbing because you have God. With God, you are the majority. I encourage you to develop a hunger and thirst for God and the things of God and let nothing or no one cause you to lose it. Only what is given by God is truly fulfilling and everlasting. Everything else is temporary.

In your time with God today, ask God to search your heart and remove any desires that would keep you from having a strong relationship with Him. Ask God to fill you with His righteousness. Honor God for being your creator, for saving your soul, for always being ready to help and guide you. Desire to draw closer to God in this moment of prayer. Open your mind, spirit, and soul to receive from God. Who knows, God may be making plans to give you your heart's desires.

DAY 3 – MEDITATION

Read the following scripture and meditate on its words before answering the question that follows. Remember to end this session in prayer with God.

Mark 8:36 (KJV)
For what shall it profit a man, if he shall gain the whole world, and lose his own soul?

What does this scripture mean to you?

_____

_____

_____

_____

_____

_____

_____

_____

_____

_____

_____

_____

_____

CONGRATULATIONS!

You have completed 1/3 of the love letters. I am confident that if you have been completely honest with God and totally submissive to God, then you are feeling more motivated and empowered than when you began this journey. More importantly, you are feeling closer to God.

If you have taken longer than the expected 12 days to get to this point, don't be hard on yourself. Keep your determination to be closer to God. Keep striving. God will honor your sincere desire to see this mission through.

DON'T GIVE UP.

PART 2

I Will Trust in You, Oh Lord

Though sorrow knocks upon my heart's door,
I will trust in you, oh Lord.
Though hurt will try to swallow me whole,
I will trust in you, oh Lord.
Though fear seeks to board my mind's train of thought,
I will trust in you oh Lord.

Though doubt creeps in to kidnap my hope,
I will trust in you oh Lord.
Though impatience pursues me day to day,
I will trust in you oh Lord.
Though people may reply "No" to my dreams, my ambitions, my heart's
desires,
I will trust in you oh Lord.

Though the weapons form, I am not defeated.
Though the winds howl, and the lightning and thunder laugh at me,
I yet stand firm, rooted in you, my Lord.
Unshakeable-Unmovable
Though darkness kidnaps my sunlight, I am yet victorious.
For you, oh Lord, are my shield, my buckler.
You, oh Lord, are all I need.
In you will I trust.

Proverbs 3:5-6 (KJV)

5 Trust in the LORD with all thine heart; and lean not unto
  thine own understanding.
6 In all thy ways acknowledge him, and he shall direct thy
  paths.

THINK ABOUT THIS...

Whenever we're faced with problems of any kind, we usually succumb to one of the following: fear, anger, worry, or calling a friend or family member. Of these options, the only one that would be beneficial in any way is reaching out to a friend or family member. Still, fear, anger, or worry could linger. How do we combat these emotions? How do we maintain our composure, our joy, our strength, our hope? The answer: Trust in God. Only God can direct us in the right direction. When we try fixing things on our own, when we depend on our own feeble-minded thinking, and when we doubt God, we mess things up. We must trust God, listen for His instructions, and act in faith. Now, I must warn you. Sometimes God's instructions might seem, well, a little crazy to you. Sometimes you might doubt you heard God correctly. Note that God's ways and thoughts are far above our own. God knows all and can see us through every obstacle that unfolds before us. All He wants is for us to trust Him.

Romans 8:28 (KJV) says, "And we know that all things work together for good to them that love God, to them who are the called according to his purpose." Yes, the good, the bad, and the frustrating are all working for your good if you have given your life to God. God does not desire that His children be defeated in any way. I encourage you to trust God in the face of oppositions, and with every decision you make. Doing so allows His peace to rule in your life.

Take this time in prayer with God. Surrender your will to God's will. Release every distraction and concern to God right now. You'll be glad you did.

DAY 2 – REFLECTION

TASKS:

1. Reflect on how you react to problems. What is your usual reaction? Did you do more harm than good?

_____

_____

_____

_____

_____

_____

_____

2. Think about how often you sought God's direction compared to when you didn't. Write it down the times you wished you had sought God.

_____

_____

_____

_____

_____

_____

Take this time to talk to God and ask God to give you the courage to seek Him first. Finally, be appreciative of God for making Himself available every time you need Him.

DAY 3 – MEDITATION

Read the following scripture and meditate on its words before answering the question that follows. Remember to end this session in prayer with God.

2 Corinthians 4:8-10 (KJV)

8We are troubled on every side, yet not distressed; we are perplexed, but not in despair;

9 Persecuted, but not forsaken; cast down, but not destroyed;

10 Always bearing about in the body the dying of the Lord Jesus, that the life also of Jesus might be made manifest in our body.

What do these scriptures mean to you when thinking about how you should react in the face of adversity?

_____

_____

_____

_____

_____

_____

_____

_____

_____

_____

Oh, How I Love You

Oh, how I love you oh Lord.
Oh, how I love you so.
Oh, how I honor you oh Lord.
I honor you so.
Oh, how I need you oh Lord.
Oh, how I need you so.
Oh, how I trust you Oh Lord.
I trust you so.

Here am I. I surrender all.
Here am I. Here am I.
Here am I. I give myself to you.
Here am I. Here am I.

No other can love me like you.
No other can comfort me like you.
No other can heal me like you.
No other can deliver me like you.
Like you, oh Lord, like you.
Like you, oh Lord, like you.

Oh, how I love you oh Lord.
Oh, how I love you so.
Oh, how I honor you oh Lord.
I honor you so.
Oh, how I need you oh Lord.
Oh, how I need you so.
Oh, how I trust you oh Lord.
I trust you so.

Psalm 118:28 (KJV)-
Thou art my God, and I will praise thee: thou art my God, I will exalt thee.

THINK ABOUT THIS...

Almost every day we are telling someone how much we appreciate or love them. We are giving them kudos for what they have done for us. If someone went out of their way to make us feel special, we would tell them how much we appreciated it. Surprise Party? "Thank you!" A Get Well Soon card? "Thank you!" A phone call to check on me? "I appreciate you!" Just because? "Thank you! You're the best!" I could go on displaying examples of how we show our appreciation to people. But how often do we show our appreciation to God? How often do we talk God up to God, let alone others? When was the last time you let God know how wonderful He is and how much you appreciate Him? When was the last time you put everything else aside and opened your heart to God to exalt His name, to magnify His name, to extol Him?

No one does more for us than God. Even when we forget about God, He doesn't forget about us. Way after way is made for us by God. God is always there for His children. The scripture James 1:17(KJV) says, "Every good gift and every perfect gift is from above, and cometh down from the Father of lights, with whom is no variableness, neither shadow of turning." Now why wouldn't you be grateful for and always ready to extend your appreciation to a God like that?

I encourage you to take this moment of prayer to thank God for all He has done for you and your loved ones. Thank God for the miracles you've seen him perform in your life and theirs. In addition, thank God for what He's done for those you don't know. Don't just focus on those closest to you or yourself. You will be blessed all the more for it.

DAY 2 - REFLECTION

TASKS:

1. List the names of people you appreciate and why you appreciate them.

_____

_____

_____

_____

_____

_____

_____

2. You have already been tasked to think of God's goodness in your life. Now, think about what God has done for you since you have begun this journey. Write it below.

_____

_____

_____

_____

_____

_____

_____

_____

How often do you thank God for his mercy, grace, unconditional love, and day-to-day strength? If this is not a habit, then I want to encourage you to make it one. Thank God for all He has allowed you to learn and accomplish. Thank God for what you have. Also, thank God for what you don't have. This could be a life-threatening disease, difficult children, difficult working conditions, horrible in-laws, unfaithful spouse, and the list goes on. There are many types of struggles you don't have. Be grateful for it.

Take this time to tell God how wonderful He is. Love on God with your words of adoration and appreciation. He's listening.

DAY 3 - MEDITATION

Read the following scripture and meditate on its words before answering the question that follows. Remember to end this session in prayer with God.

1 Thessalonians 5:18 (KJV)
In everything give thanks: for this is the will of God in Christ Jesus concerning you.

What does this scripture mean to you when thinking about giving thanks and showing appreciation to God?

_____

_____

_____

_____

_____

_____

_____

_____

_____

_____

_____

_____

_____

I Surrender

I surrender my fears and worries. I surrender my hate and strife.
I surrender my frustrations and anguish.
I surrender my soul, my life.

I surrender my hurt and pain and all my sorrows too.
I surrender everything that weighs me down.
Lord, I surrender them all to you.

Fill me with your joy, Lord. Fill me with your peace and love.
Open up the mighty floodgates of Heaven above.

Pour out your spirit my God, and let it rest on me.
Rejuvenate my tired soul.
Come and set me free.

To reverence and please you, Lord, are my heart's desire.
Please meet my request, have mercy on me.
Lord, take me higher.

Higher in you, oh Lord, higher in you, standing on solid ground.
Never to turn away from you,
Never to turn around.

Never to return to sin again and never to drought or lack.
I surrender to you, my Lord, my God.
I refuse to ever turn back.

Matthew 16: 24-25 (KJV)

24 Then said Jesus unto his disciples, if any man will come after me, let him deny himself, and take up his cross, and follow me.

25 For whosoever will save his life shall lose it: and whosoever will lose his life for my sake shall find it.

THINK ABOUT THIS...

Our desire to get closer to someone usually comes with the need to give something up. Sometimes, we give up time spent with family or friends, or it could be time spent taking care of responsibilities. What we surrender may be a personal desire that we deem less important than being able to build that relationship. This is especially true when we become romantically interested in someone. In any relationship, sacrifice is inevitable. The same is true when we desire to build a relationship with God.

What must we give up in order to have a strong, close relationship with God? It's simple, but somehow, we make it difficult. God asks that we surrender our lives to Him. He desires that we surrender our sinful ways, our struggles, our worries, and our doubts. We can't love God and expect to build a strong relationship with Him if we choose to live a life of sin or distrust. (I believe we've been down this trust road before.) In addition, we need to surrender our gifts, talents, and every possession to God. They exist only because of God, and we must make it a point to use them for God's glory.

One other point I need to make is that we must exchange our will for God's will. We have many desires, but God's desire for our lives far outweigh ours. What God has planned for us will bring us more peace, joy and happiness than we could ever imagine. We just need to say, "Thy will be done." Jesus did, and He came out victoriously. He conquered sin and death.

At this time, give your all to God in prayer. Pray now that God helps you surrender everything to Him.

DAY 2 - REFLECTION

TASKS:

1. Get a clean sheet of paper and list everything you are concerned about: fears, stressors, sorrows, griefs, doubts, etc. Now, lift this list toward Heaven and tell God, "They are yours. I surrender them all to you, Lord." Finally, place the list in your Bible by Psalms 55:22 (KJV) "Cast thy burden upon the LORD, and he shall sustain thee: he shall never suffer the righteous to be moved."

2. List all your gifts, talents, and possessions. Place a star next to the ones you use for God's glory. If you find you are slacking in this area, simply begin today with seeking God on how you can use what you listed to honor Him.

_____

_____

_____

_____

_____

_____

_____

_____

_____

_____

3. Write down your dreams and ambitions and why you desire them.

_____

_____

_____

_____

_____

_____

_____

_____

_____

_____

Today, you have identified areas in your life that you can surrender to God. You have identified your gifts and possessions and noted whether you use them for God's glory. Finally, you wrote down your dreams and ambitions along with your reasons for each of them. Right now, I want you to take a closer look at the latter. Are your desires for selfish gain? Do these ambitions line up with God's will for your life? It goes back to surrendering everything. Surrendering to God will draw you closer to Him and help you seek after the right dreams and ambitions. When what we desire lines up with God's will, God's perfect plan for our lives can unfold.

Now, I encourage you to let go of your will and grab hold of God's will. Let go and take hold of a life filled with victory in the face of opposition, hope in the face of hopelessness, joy in the face of sorrow, peace in the midst of turmoil, and love in the face of hate. Pray and ask God to take away selfishness and give you a heart filled with His love and righteousness. Ask God to help you desire the things of God, to desire a life that brings glory to His name.

DAY 3 – MEDITATION

Read the following scripture and meditate on its words before answering the question that follows. Remember to end this session in prayer with God.

Romans 12: 1-2 (KJV)

₁I beseech you therefore, brethren, by the mercies of God, that ye present your bodies a living sacrifice, holy, acceptable unto God, which is your reasonable service.

₂And be not conformed to this world: but be ye transformed by the renewing of your mind, that ye may prove what is that good, and acceptable, and perfect, will of God.

What does this passage of scripture mean to you in relation to surrendering your life to God?

_____

_____

_____

_____

_____

_____

_____

_____

_____

_____

_____

_____

_____

Most Holy One

You hear my cry. You hear my plea.

Every time that I need thee.

You comfort my soul. You fill my heart.

Draw near to me and never depart.

Upon my knees I humbly bow.

I welcome your presence in right now.

You are my refuge, my strength the day long.

You are my joy, my love song.

I worship and honor you. I reverence your name.

In you I am made whole. There's no room for shame.

Without you I'm lost, a wondering soul.

Together - with you I'm complete - whole.

Take charge of my life. Thy will be done.

My faithful God - Most Holy One.

Psalm 71:22 (KJV)

I will also praise thee with the psaltery, even thy truth, O my God: unto thee will I sing with the harp, O thou Holy One of Israel.

THINK ABOUT THIS...

Your creator is not a dictator. He is not a slave master. He is not a man that He would lie (Numbers 23:19, KJV). God desires to love you unconditionally. He is always available to listen, comfort, protect, direct, and encourage. Whatever you need God to be to you and for you, that He will be. God will be your strength. God will be your joy, TRUE JOY. God will be your best friend. God will be a husband or wife, a mother or father. Do you need a doctor or a lawyer? God will be that too. Why wouldn't you want to take time to honor God when He is always available to be there for you? Good question, huh? God is holy. God is faithful. God is merciful. God is righteous. God has no favorites.

Take this moment to welcome God into your presence. Love on God with your words. Love on God with a song. Pour out praise and worship to the Lord God Most High. Reverence His holy name, and watch God move supernaturally.

DAY 2 - REFLECTION

TASKS:

1. Reflect upon your life. When have you allowed God to work, and where did you not allowed God to work?

_____

_____

_____

_____

_____

_____

_____

2. Reflect on your current state. Where are you allowing God to work? Where are you trying to handle the matter on your own?

_____

_____

_____

_____

_____

_____

Let God be everything you need. Thank Him for all that He has already been and is currently being in your life. Acknowledge that you are because of God. You have because of God. God is and has always been everything you need. God IS the Most Holy One.

Reread the letter, and as you are doing so, open your heart fully to God and love on Him. Let God know how much you appreciate Him being there to provide what you need. This letter may not cover everything God has been to you, so call it all out. Acknowledge God in every area of your life. Reverence Him now and lose yourself in song, in praise, in worship. Draw closer and closer and even closer to God. Leave no space between you and God for even air to fill. God's waiting.

DAY 3 – MEDITATION

Read the following passage scripture and meditate on its words before answering the question that follows. Remember to end this session in prayer with God.

Psalms 145: 17-21(KJV)

17 The LORD is righteous in all his ways, and holy in all his works.

18 The LORD is nigh unto all them that call upon him, to all that call upon him in truth.

19 He will fulfil the desire of them that fear him: he also will hear their cry and will save them.

20 The LORD preserveth all them that love him: but all the wicked will he destroy.

21 My mouth shall speak the praise of the LORD: and let all flesh bless his holy name for ever and ever.

What does this passage of scripture mean to you as you think about God's holiness and God's works?

_____

_____

_____

_____

_____

_____

_____

_____

_____

_____

CONGRATULATIONS!

You have completed the second third of the book. You are just over halfway to the end of your journey. By now I am sure your trust in God has increased, as well as your love and appreciation for Him.

Again, if you have fallen behind, don't stop. Continue to the end. Keep pressing. Keep pushing. Keep striving. With every step of determination and faith, you are becoming more and more victorious. Remember, nothing worth having comes easy.

VICTORY AWAITS AT THE END!

PART 3

Hide Me Under Your Shadow

Hide me under your shadow.
Let me still away with you.
Wrap your loving arms around me.
Pull me close to you.

Wipe the tears from my bloodshot eyes.
Comfort my weary soul.
Gather my broken pieces and make me whole.

Hide me under your shadow.
Protect me all day long.
Guard my heart and mind, so I do no wrong.

Light the way out of darkness. Order every step I take.
Grab hold the chains that bind me.
And cause them all to break.

Hide me under your shadow. Enjoy my songs of praise.
Receive my holy worship.
I give to you always.

Be exalted. Be extoled.
Be reverenced and glorified.
Hide me under your shadow.
Keep me eternally by your side.

Psalm 91:1-2 (KJV)

1 He that dwelleth in the secret place of the Most High shall abide under the shadow of the Almighty.

2 I will say of the LORD, He is my refuge and my fortress: my God; in him will I trust.

53

THINK ABOUT THIS...

We all long to feel safe, comforted, and protected. We look for these securities from family, friends, coworkers, and even technologies. Yet, neither of these are 100% guarantees. Neither of these come with a fail-safe. There is always a chance they will let us down. Thankfully, there is one on whom we can lean and depend and who will never fail us. God can be trusted with everything. God has no limits that would keep Him from being able to protect us and comfort us in our time of need. He sits with HIs arms wide open, ready to wrap us up at any given moment. God's love for His children is never-ending. He has a secret place for all of them to dwell safely with Him. This place deters fear, discouragement, shame, stress, anxiety, depression, worry, sorrow, and anything else that would weigh us down and keep us from enjoying a fruitful life.

Take this time to seek God for whatever type of protection you need. God is only a prayer away. Remember to thank God for the protection He has already provided. Let this time with God be filled with thanksgiving as well as supplication.

DAY 2 - REFLECTION

TASKS:

1. List everyone you depend or have depended on for one reason or another and why. Put an **X** next to the ones that did not work out well for you.

_____

_____

_____

_____

_____

_____

_____

2. List every item (tool or machine) you depended on for one reason or another and why. Put an **X** next to the ones that did not work out well for you.

_____

_____

_____

_____

_____

_____

_____

_____

I'm sure at one time or another you were disappointed by someone or something you just knew would be helpful or supportive. It has happened to all of us. Think about how depending on God instead of that person might have changed the outcome. Of course, tools and machinery will fail at some point during their use. But often times, we put more trust in people than God. Why? They are visible. They are tangible. Trusting in people we see and know personally gives us a sense of security. This same sense of security can be found in God if we only make the conscious effort to get to know Him better.

The point of this entire book is to help you draw closer to God. To help guide you to a place in God you have never traveled. To help you experience God on a whole new level. If you have allowed yourself to do just that up to this point, then you should be feeling quite secure in God. If you're not there yet, don't give up. Don't be discouraged. If you truly want to fall in love with God and walk closely with Him, then you will. This journey isn't a quick drying cement or a microwave dinner. This is a journey of perseverance and determination because Satan is always ready to ensure you don't reach your goal. Are you going to let him stop you? Would you let anyone or anything else keep you from reaching your goals? I think not. So, why let Satan?

Go ahead and rest in the secret place God has set aside just for you. Let God wrap you up, and while He's doing so let His voice comfort you and direct you. Let God's voice soothe your spirit and take you to a level of peace you've never experienced. Close your eyes, lift your hands towards Heaven, and surrender yourself to God. Listen for His soft, gentle voice. God is speaking. Listen and still away with Him.

DAY 3 – MEDITATION

Read the following division of Psalms and meditate on its words before answering the question that follows. Remember to end this session in prayer with God.

Psalms 121 (KJV)

1 I will lift up mine eyes unto the hills, from whence cometh my help.
2 My help cometh from the LORD, which made heaven and earth.
3 He will not suffer thy foot to be moved: he that keepeth thee will not slumber.
4 Behold, he that keepeth Israel shall neither slumber nor sleep.
5 The LORD is thy keeper: the LORD is thy shade upon thy right hand.
6 The sun shall not smite thee by day, nor the moon by night.
7 The LORD shall preserve thee from all evil: he shall preserve thy soul.
8 The LORD shall preserve thy going out and thy coming in from this time forth, and even for evermore.

What does this passage of scripture mean to you when thinking about God's provisions in your life?

_____

_____

_____

_____

_____

_____

_____

_____

_____

_____

No Better Place

There's no better place in the whole wide world
that's better than being with you, Lord.

There's no better place to find peace.
There's no better place to find comfort.
There's no better place to find strength.
There's no better place to find joy.
There no better place than with you, Lord.

There's no better place to find love.
There's no better place to find answers.
There's no better place to find friendship.
There's no better place to find everything I need.
There's no better place than with you, Lord.

Nothing can compare to your presence.
Nothing can compare to being wrapped in your arms.
Being held by you-Being loved unconditionally.
There's no better place than with you, Lord.
There's no better place than with you.

Hold me. Console me. Wrap me in your arms.
Allow me to rest there, God, from the craziness of the world.
Hold me. Console me. Wrap me in your arms.
Let me rest there, God, from the pressures of life.
Hold me. Console me.
Lord, wrap me in your arms.

Let me rest there.

-FOREVER-

Psalm 62:8 (KJV) Trust in him at all times; ye people, pour out your heart before him: God is a refuge for us. Selah.

THINK ABOUT THIS...

It is human nature to want to enjoy the company of another person or group of people. Many of us like to entertain company or be entertained. We find pleasure in laughing and dancing and talking with friends, family, or even co-workers. It's in our DNA. But what about enjoying God's company? What about "entertaining" God? How often do you make time to get into the presence of God to allow Him to shower you with His love?

By now, you should be in a place where spending time with God has become second-natured. If you have been consistent on this journey, you have spent time with God every day for almost a month. If you haven't been consistent, don't let it discourage you. Keep on pressing.

Regardless of where you are on this journey, end this session with God. Talk to Him. Open yourself up to what God has to say to you today.

DAY 2 - REFLECTION

TASK:

Write down you daily schedule. Did you include your time with God? If not, include it. Your journey is almost over. Be mindful that you don't let this consistent time with God end.

_____

_____

_____

_____

_____

_____

_____

_____

_____

The need to spend time in God's presence can be compared to our need for oxygen, water, and food. In order to be spiritually strong, in order to be spiritually alive, we must make time for God. We must be determined to spend time in His presence. It is there we can be rejuvenated, refreshed, awakened, enlightened, comforted, and loved.

Use this moment to spend time with God. Go ahead. Talk to Him. Let God take you into His arms and hold you, console you, and comfort you. Rest there for a while. It's the best place you can be.

DAY 3 – MEDITATION

Read the following scripture and meditate on what it is saying before answering the question that follows. Remember to end this session in prayer with God.

Psalm 16:11 (KJV)
Thou wilt shew me the path of life: in thy presence is fulness of joy; at thy right hand there are pleasures for evermore

What does this scripture mean to you when considering the importance of spending time with God and getting into the presence of God?

_____

_____

_____

_____

_____

_____

_____

_____

_____

_____

_____

_____

Where...

Where is true peace?

I find it in you.

Where is joy overflowing?

It flows from you.

Where is strength?

I receive it from you.

Where is comfort?

It's given by you.

Where is hope?

I find it in you.

Where is love?

It IS you.

Where is patience?

I learn it from you.

Where is victory?

It's because of you.

Where is everything I need?

Lord it's in you and only you.

Philippians 4:19 (KJV)-

But my God shall supply all your need according to his riches in glory by Christ Jesus.

THINK ABOUT THIS...

Throughout life we seek love, joy, peace, strength, and direction from various sources: people, the internet, books, magazines, newspapers, and the list goes on. While these sources may yield what we want, the amount yielded is limited. The love may be conditional. The joy and peace are temporary and artificial. The strength is limited, and the direction is unclear and sometimes filled with obstacles that could have been avoided.

The unconditional love we seek can only be found in God. He gave his only son to die for our sins. In Him, we can find true joy that the world can never give us, a peace that no one can understand, a strength that can withstand the worst of circumstances, and directions that are so clear we could walk the path blindfolded.

As you enter into prayer with God, release to God any concerns you may have at this time. Allow your heart to receive the fullness of His blessings. Be comforted. Be restored. Be encouraged. Be strengthened. Be filled with God's peace.

DAY 2 - REFLECTION

TASKS:

1. Think about where you look for love, joy, peace, and direction. List your sources below.

_____

_____

_____

_____

_____

_____

_____

_____

_____

Analyze your list. At this point on your journey, God should have been listed. Hopefully God was written first. If you discover that you have been looking for a need in a place other than God, try God. God is always ready to help us. He will supply whatever we need when we need it.

Philippians 4:6-7 tells us to let our request be made know to God, and His peace that surpasses all understanding will keep our hearts and minds through Christ Jesus. So, as you enter into prayer, be sure to let God know EVERYTHING you need from Him. God wants you to confess it. God wants you to lean on Him.

DAY 3 – MEDITATION

Read the following passage of scripture and meditate on what it is saying before answering the question that follows. Be sure to end this session in prayer with God.

Matthew 7: 7-8,11 (KJV)

7 Ask, and it shall be given you; seek, and ye shall find; knock, and it shall be opened unto you:

8 For every one that asketh receiveth; and he that seeketh findeth; and to him that knocketh it shall be opened.

11 If ye then, being evil, know how to give good gifts unto your children, how much more shall your Father which is in heaven give good things to them that ask him?

What does this passage of scripture mean to you when considering that God is where you can find everything you need?

_____

_____

_____

_____

_____

_____

_____

_____

_____

To Behold You

I hear you-
In rushing rivers hurrying along,
In streams meandering the forest floors,
In a dog's bark, a cat's meow,
In the roar of a lion, a wolf's howl,

In a songbird's melody, the quack of a duck,
In the croak of a frog, a woodpecker pecking,
In a thunderous clap shaking the atmosphere,
And in the pounding of rain upon Earth's surface,

I also hear you-
In the crash of ocean waves along the shore,
In the shaking of earth's ground,
In the explosion of a volcanoes top,
In the thunderous roar of an avalanche,

In the whistling winds singing their song,
In the trickling sounds of a stream,
In the rustling of leaves waving to all who pass,
And in the stillness of the air.

I feel you-
In gentle breezes so crisp and cool,
In the sun's rays warming the land,
In Winter's artic breath icing the waters,
In Summer's heat waves cooking the air,

In the coolness of a river's waters,
In the warmth of a sunbaked stone,
In the softness of the meadow's grass,
And in the gentle grit of sandy beaches.

I also feel you-

In the poke of a desert cactus,
In the prick of a rose's thorn,
In the roughness of a tree's bark,
In the smoothness of a pebble,

In the joy of a baby's birth,
In the hugs and kisses of a mother,
In the protection given by a father,
And in the prayers of a wise pastor.

I see you-

As the sun rises and when it sets,
In puffs of clouds or a clear blue sky,
On a moonlit evening,
Or a starry night,

In trees dancing in the breeze,
In the flowers coating the meadows,
On a mountain top blanketed with snow,
And deep in the painted valleys.

I also see you-

In nature's ponds decorated with ripples,
In the foggy mist hovering above them,
In an iceberg giant and snow-covered tundra,
In the dunes of sand and the deserts hot and dry,

In butterflies and birds navigating the airways,
In ants bustling about,
In herds roaming the open plains,
And in fish freely swimming along.

I can also see you-

In snowflakes dotting the air,
In a raindrop resting on a flower's petal,
In a lightning bolt dancing amongst the heavens,
In the looming dark clouds swelled with moisture.

In the glistening waters of a lake,
In the sparkle of a hidden gem,
In the sunrays streaming through the woods,
And in a rainbow anchored in the sky.

Lord, how wonderful it is to hear you!
How comforting it is to feel you!
How marvelous it is to see you!
How amazing it is to behold you!

Genesis 1:1-2 (KJV)
1In the beginning God created the heaven and the earth.
2And the earth was without form, and void; and darkness was upon the face of the deep. And the Spirit of God moved upon the face of the waters.

THINK ABOUT THIS...

Everything in the world around us was created by God. God is even in the midst of miracles and the unconditional love shown to us by others. God is everywhere. Unfortunately, life can have us so caught up that we forget to hear, feel, and see God around us.

In the beginning of everything, God was there. At the start of life, God was there. As creation was occurring, God was there. Today, God is still there… here…EVERYWHERE. Make the time to stop and observe His marvelous works.

As you enter into prayer, think about the beauty around you. Thank God for creating it. Think about the beautiful people God has placed around you. Thank God for them. Be even more thankful in your prayer to God today. God is so very deserving of it. Don't you agree?

DAY 2 - REFLECTION

TASKS:

1. Write down the average time you take in one week to just rest from all the hustle and bustle of your life.

    _____

2. Write down the number of vacations you take in a year. Hopefully, you have at least one.

    _____

3. Write down the average number of times you take to admire God's beautiful artwork in the world around you.

    _____

"Stop and smell the roses" is a very well-known phrase. To me, it's something we all should strive to do. Stop for a moment and enjoy what's around you, enjoy life. How often do you take a break from the chaos in your life? How often do you take a moment just for you? Sometimes it's not often enough. When we do take those moments, we feel so good. Taking time for ourselves is vital to surviving mentally, physically, and most importantly, spiritually.

Likewise, we need to take the time to recognize God around us. Seeing God's hand in the beauty of nature, and even in the not so beautiful, can give us a greater appreciation for the One who created it all. Allowing yourself to feel

71

God, hear God, and see God in the world around you can draw you closer to Him. You begin to remember how marvelous God is, how powerful God is, and how excellent God is. And then, you can't help but love God even more.

If you have never (or rarely) take the time to hear, feel, and see God around you, I invite you to do so now. Look out your window, or better yet, go outside. Listen. Feel. Observe. Walk your neighborhood, hike, or stroll along a beach or in a park. Allow God to open your eyes, your heart, and your spirit. Allow God to draw you even closer to Him.

DAY 3 – MEDITATION

Read the following passages of scripture and meditate on what they are saying before answering the question that follows. Be sure to end this session in prayer with God.

Jeremiah 32:17 (KJV)
Ah Lord God! Behold, thou hast made the heaven and the earth by thy great power and stretched out arm, and there is nothing too hard for thee.

John 1:3 (KJV)
All things were made by him; and without him was not anything made that was made.

What do these scriptures mean to you in relation to seeing God all around us?

_____

_____

_____

_____

_____

_____

_____

_____

_____

_____

FINAL REFLECTION

Congratulations! You have completed your journey to building and strengthening your relationship with God. But, your journey is not complete. Your journey is never complete. You should make a point to stay in constant communication with God. It's not easy. But do your best to keep the lines of communication between you and God opened.

At this time, reflect on what you have gained from this journey. At the start, you were asked to write down goals you hoped to achieve and why. Look back at your list. Did you achieve all of your goals? If not, why? Make note of your reflection below.

_____

_____

_____

_____

_____

_____

_____

_____

_____

_____

_____

_____

_____

_____

NEXT STEPS

In order to meet goals, a plan must be implemented. If you had goals you did not achieve, ask God to show you how to achieve them. Maybe you have discovered other achievements you would like to accomplish. Ask God to show you how to achieve them as well. Take time to write down your goals and plans to meet each goal. In addition, include a plan on how you will ensure you continue making time for God. If there is one relationship worth your time and effort, it's your relationship with your creator.

_____

_____

_____

_____

_____

_____

_____

_____

_____

_____

_____

_____

_____

_____

_____

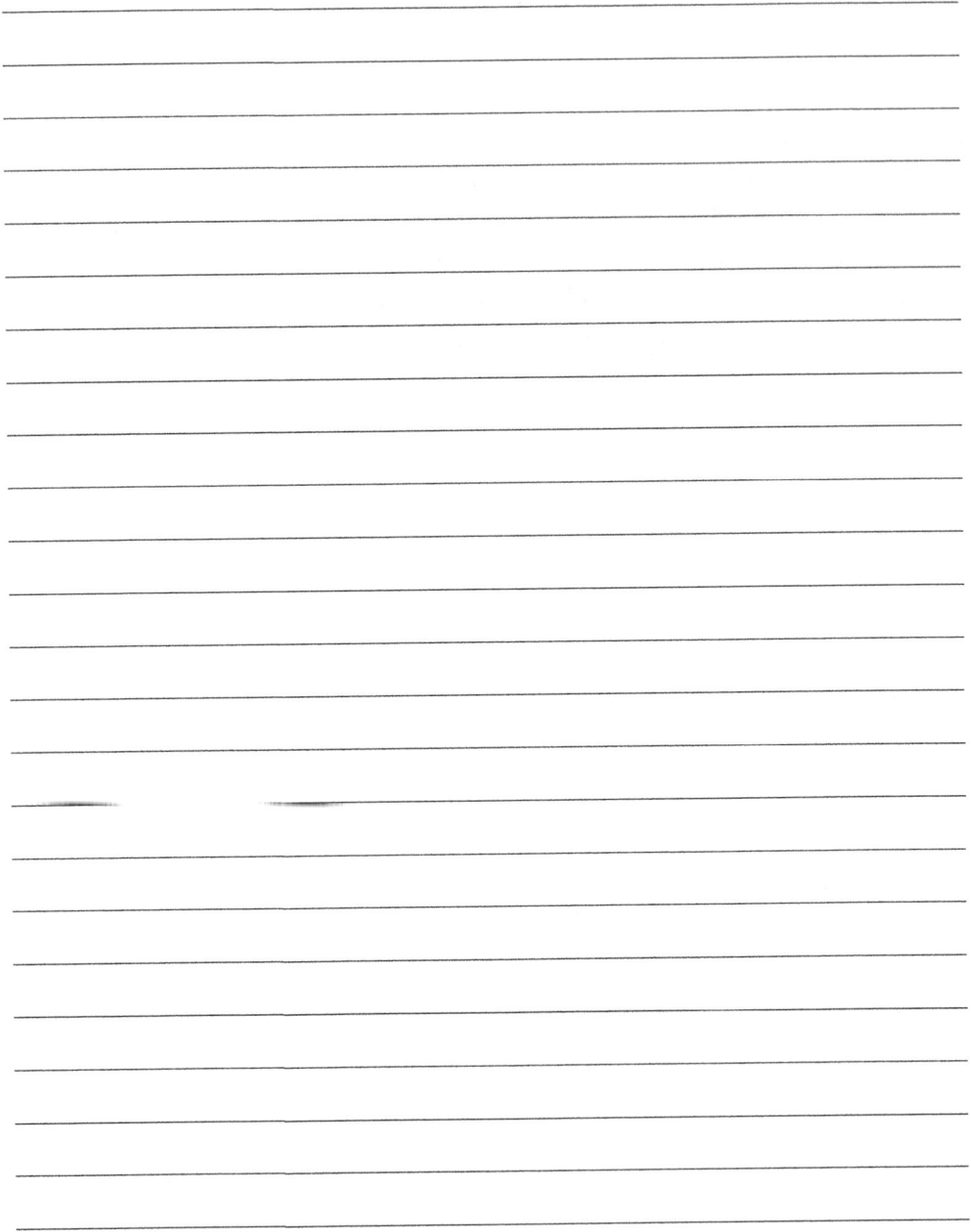

FINAL WORDS

You started this journey with a focus on recognizing God's love for you. God sent Jesus to die for the sins of the world. Jesus died for those who came before him, those there during his lifespan, and those who came after him.

Your journey continued with a call to reflect on God's greatness, encouraging you to hunger for His righteousness, surrender to His will, and allow Him to care for you as He so desires. In addition, you were charged to look for everything you need and desire in God. It is my hope that you have chosen to do each of these tasks. More importantly, it is my hope you continue to love on God and allow God to love on you.

Finally, your journey led you to a place of recognizing God around you. You were charged with looking at your surroundings from a different perspective with the understanding of God as Creator. Everything He created serves a purpose and is set in its perfect place with its perfect function. This includes you. God has a purpose for your life. He desires for you to prosper in spite of the turmoil you may face. You are God's greatest creation. No matter what, God loves you unconditionally.

Take the time to still away with God and to see God working around you. Remember, building and strengthening your relationship with God is the most important task for you to do every day. Simply put, it's a matter of life or death-mentally, physically, and spiritually.

God Bless You,
Evangelist Stroud

About the Author

I am a mother of three amazing young men, Julius IV, Jhan, and Jordan. I have been married to the most wonderful man, Julius III for 26 years. He is truly my knight in shining armor. In addition to being an Evangelist for God, I am an elementary school teacher, and I've enjoyed my profession for 20 years.

As for my spiritual walk, since I gave my life to Christ, my journey can best be described as a roller coaster ride. It has not always been easy, but that's life. Right? God never promised us a life without struggles, without opposition, without sorrows, without disappointments, or without anything tragedy. But what God did promise was to be there every time we need Him.

I can honestly say that my relationship with God saved me. My relationship with God is the reason that I am not in an asylum, in jail, or dead. Whenever I was ready to give up or give in to the unthinkable thoughts that were presented to me (by no one but Satan of course), I could feel God's loving arms wrap around me. I could hear God's soothing voice speaking to me. Had I never made up in my mind to start, nurture, and strengthen my relationship with God, I wouldn't have been able to feel His presence and hear His voice in those crucial moments. Those moments were crossroads I had approached on my journey through life. The decisions I chose to make would define my future. Knowing God and making the choice to continually commune with Him helped me make the right choices.

I wrote this book from my heart and with the strong desire that everyone who reads it will live a life full of God's joy, peace, and love. It is my prayer every reader of *Love Letters to God* will experience a greater presence of God

around them and will be empowered to say, "NO!" to every negative thought and lie presented to them because they realize God is standing next to them ready to fight for them... ready to protect them... ready to free them... ready to love them unconditionally. They can say, "NO!" because they realize God's way is ALWAYS the best way.

Additional Notes

References

All scriptures within this book were taken from the King James Version of the Bible.

Made in the USA
Coppell, TX
01 April 2020